by Kathryn Corbett
illustrated by Dave Blanchett

Harcourt

Orlando   Boston   Dallas   Chicago   San Diego

Visit *The Learning Site!*

www.harcourtschool.com

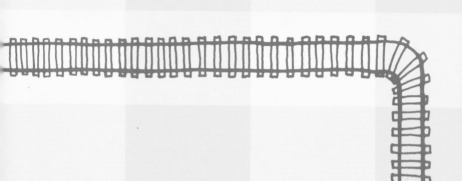

Raccoon was feeling sad because
His engine wouldn't run.
It wouldn't pull his little train.
Raccoon could not have fun.

3

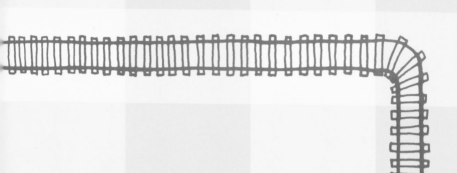

"I just can't fix this engine.
I don't know why it broke.
It will not sing its chug-chug song
Or make its puffs of smoke."

4

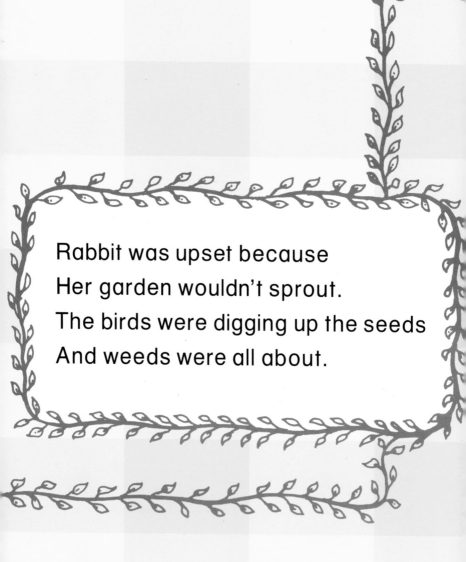

Rabbit was upset because
Her garden wouldn't sprout.
The birds were digging up the seeds
And weeds were all about.

"I like to grow a garden,
But not to dig or weed.
It's really hard to do the chores
Without the tools I need."

Rabbit left her garden
And went to see Raccoon.
She said, "I'll fix your engine.
We'll have it working soon."

"Fixing something broken
Is a simple job for me.
I will fix your train set—
You just wait and see!"

"I'll bring my fixing tools and work
Right alongside you.
We will fix your engine.
It may just need some glue."

Rabbit sat next to Raccoon
And showed him what to do.
They took apart the engine
And made it run like new.

"Rabbit, thanks! I learned a lot!"
Raccoon said with a cheer.
"Now let's make your garden sprout
I have the tools right here."

Raccoon and Rabbit turned the dirt.

They pulled out all the weeds.

They made a scarecrow so the birds

Would not eat up the seeds.

They gathered up the garden tools,
And Rabbit thanked her friend.
"Raccoon, you'll have some
ears of corn
Before the summer's end."

Both jobs now seemed so simple.
Everything was done.
When good friends help each other,
Their chores can seem like fun!